Project Fluffy

THE INFAMOUS RATSOS

Project Fluffy

Kara LaReau

illustrated by Matt Myers

CANDLEWICK PRESS

Text copyright © 2018 by Kara LaReau
Illustrations copyright © 2018 by Matt Myers

First edition 2018

Library of Congress Catalog Card Number pending
ISBN 978-1-5362-0005-8

18 19 20 21 22 23 LSC 10 9 8 7 6 5 4 3 2 1

Printed in Crawfordsville, IN, U.S.A.

This book was typeset in Scala.
The illustrations were done in ink and watercolor dye on paper.

Candlewick Press
99 Dover Street
Somerville, Massachusetts 02144

visit us at www.candlewick.com

MIX
Paper from
responsible sources
FSC
www.fsc.org FSC® C132124

For Scott, who is the dreamiest

K. L.

For Darrell, my lifelong and true friend

M. M.

EVERYONE LOVES CHUCK

ATTENTION, STUDENTS!" Principal Otteriguez announces to the lunchroom. "In honor of Poetry Month, Peter Rabbit Elementary will be holding its first annual poetry contest!"

"Poetry?" says Chad Badgerton.

"*Bo*-ring," says Ralphie.

"Shh," says Louie. "I can't hear what he's saying."

"First, second, and third prize will be gift certificates to Clawmart!" Mr. Otteriguez announces. "The contest ends on Thursday after school, and we'll reveal the winners next Friday!"

"Poetry is so . . . sappy," says Chad.

"Not all of it. Miss Beavers has been showing us some really funny poems," says Tiny.

"Mr. Ferretti says that poetry is about *feelings*," says Chad. "*Blech.*"

"All art is about feelings," Millicent informs him.

"And about connecting through feelings," Tiny adds. "Love, anger, joy, sadness . . ."

"Like I said," says Chad. *"Blech."*

"Well, I'm going to use *my* feelings to win that contest. In fact, I already have a plan," Louie says. He looks at Ralphie. "We'll write a poem together, and then we'll use the first-prize Clawmart gift certificate to buy ourselves skateboards!"

"Oh, boy! We've been talking about getting skateboards forever," says Ralphie. "No more walking to school. We can ride in style!"

"Are you gonna eat that?" Chad asks, pointing at Tiny's brownie.

"Go for it," says Tiny.

"I love chocolate," says Chad.

"If you love it so much, why don't you write a poem about it?" asks Ralphie.

"I don't love it *that* much," says Chad through a mouthful of brownie.

"Speaking of love . . ." says Millicent.

She looks over at Chuck Wood in the hot lunch line and bats her eyelashes. "Isn't he *dreamy?*"

"I wish I were friends with Chuck," says Tiny. "Everyone does. He's the coolest."

"Don't you think he's dreamy, Fluffy?" Millicent asks.

But Fluffy isn't listening. She's writing in her green notebook. She's been writing in it and looking through a stack of library books all through lunch.

"What are you scribbling in that thing?" Millicent asks. "Are you already working on a poem?"

"No, it's plans for my garden," Fluffy says.

"You have your own garden?" Millicent asks.

"I have my own plot in the community garden, at the Big City Park," Fluffy explains. "I want to make sure I have room for all my favorite fruits and vegetables."

"I do *not* love fruits and vegetables," says Chad.

"You're missing out," says Fluffy. "You can't just eat junk food all day."

"I can try," Chad says, licking brownie crumbs off his fingers.

Fluffy's gardening books fall off the lunch table. Chuck Wood picks them up.

"Thank you," says Fluffy.

"Gardening, huh?" says Chuck. "My grandma likes to garden."

"Gardening is not just for *grandmas*," Fluffy informs him.

"OK," says Chuck. "See you around."

"Oh, isn't he the *sweetest?*" Millicent says, sighing.

Tiny sighs, too. "And the *coolest,*" he says.

"I think it would be *cool* if you all gave me your *sweets,*" Chad says, helping himself to everyone else's brownies.

– 2 –

PROJECT FLUFFY

We only have a week to get our poem together," says Louie as the Ratso brothers walk home from school. "We'd better start right away."

"Righto," says Ralphie. "So, what should we write about?"

"Leave the thinking to me," says Louie. He considers himself the smart one.

"Hey, wait up!" says a voice behind them. It's Chuck Wood. "I thought maybe we could walk together, since I live about a block away from you guys."

"You want to walk with *us*?" says Louie. "I mean, sure. That's cool."

"I heard you're the ones who put together the Big City FunTime Arcade," Chuck says.

"Yep. We're open every Saturday morning," Louie informs him.

"You're great at planning things," says Chuck. "Do you think you could help *me* plan something?"

"Sure," says Louie. "What is it?"

Chuck looks at Ralphie, then at Louie.

"It's . . . kind of secret," he says.

"Chuck and I need to talk for a while," Louie informs his brother. *"Alone."*

"What about our poem?" Ralphie asks.

"We'll work on it later," says Louie.

Ralphie rolls his eyes. He lets them walk ahead.

"OK," says Louie. He takes his clipboard out of his backpack. "So, what's this project?"

"Well . . . it's not really a what. It's a *who*," Chuck says. "There's a girl I like, but I can't seem to get her attention. And you're friends with her."

"You mean Millicent?" Louie says. "Believe me, you have her attention."

"No, I mean the one with the glasses. And those *amazing* ears," says Chuck, sighing.

"Fluffy?" says Louie.

"Fluffy," says Chuck. He smiles. "So, do you think you can help?"

Louie is already making notes on his clipboard.

"Of course. Why don't you sit with us at lunch tomorrow?" he says. "We'll call it Phase One of Project Fluffy."

"Sounds like a plan," says Chuck.

Louie looks up from his clipboard.

"Where's my brother?" he asks.

Ralphie has taken a shortcut home. The Ratso brothers have an

after-school   routine—they   play
their favorite video game and eat
their favorite snack.

"Want to play *Verminator*?" Ralphie
asks when Louie finally gets home.

"I can't," says Louie, making Project Fluffy notes on his clipboard. "I have work to do."

"What about the poetry contest? And the skateboards?" Ralphie asks. But Louie has already gone into their room and closed the door.

Ralphie throws the bag of snacks in the trash. *These Happy Puffs are stale,* he thinks. Or maybe he's just in a not-very-happy mood.

- 3 -

SQUEEEEE!

I can't believe Chuck Wood is sitting with us!" Millicent whispers to Tiny.

"Me neither!" Tiny whispers to Millicent. "The coolest of the cool, at *our lunch table!*"

They both make a noise that sounds a lot like "SQUEEEEE!"

"You two need to chill out," says Ralphie. He sees Chad eyeing his pizza and pulls it toward himself.

"I love pizza," says Chad.

"Well, love your own pizza," says Ralphie. "This is mine."

"Start talking," Louie whispers to Chuck, giving him a nudge.

"About what?" Chuck asks.

"Let Fluffy know how cool you are," Louie says.

Chuck clears his throat. "Uh, I think I've seen you in the park before," he says to Fluffy.

"Hmm?" Fluffy says. She doesn't look up. She has her nose in her gardening notebook again.

"Usually I'm playing baseball with my team, the Big City Critters. I'm a really good pitcher," Chuck says. "You should come and watch sometime. We practice every day after school, and we have games on Saturday afternoons."

"Hmm," Fluffy says again, making some notes.

"I love baseball," Tiny says.

"Can we come and watch?" asks Millicent.

"Um, sure," says Chuck. "How about you, Fluffy?"

"What?" she asks.

"Do you want to watch me play baseball in the park?" Chuck asks.

"I don't go to the park to watch baseball," Fluffy informs him. "I go there to garden."

And then she goes back to her notebook.

Chuck looks at Louie. Louie shrugs.

"I guess it's time for Phase Two," he says.

"What's Phase Two?" asks Chuck.

"Come to my place after school," says Louie.

"Just what I need," grumbles Ralphie. "More of the Louie and Chuck Show."

"I know what *I* need," Chad says, wiggling his eyebrows.

Ralphie sighs and pushes his tray of pizza across the table.

- 4 -

WITH LOVE, CHUCKY

So, what's Phase Two?" Chuck asks back at the Ratsos' apartment.

"Forget Phase Two, when are we going to work on our poem for the contest?" Ralphie asks his brother.

"First things first," says Louie, taking out his clipboard.

"Ugh, I just can't win," Ralphie says. He turns on his video game. "Except when I'm playing *Verminator.*"

"Speaking of poems," Louie says to Chuck, "I think you should write one for Fluffy!"

"Um, I'm not really a writer," he says.

"That's OK," Louie says. "You just tell me what you want to say, and I'll do the rest."

"What I want to say? To Fluffy?" says Chuck. "I want her to like me. Everyone likes me."

"Not everyone," mumbles Ralphie.

"She should know I'm cool, and I'm fun, and I'm really good at sports," adds Chuck.

"OK, great," says Louie. He scribbles, then crosses things out.

Then he scribbles some more. Then he crumples up the paper and starts again. And again. And again.

"This is taking forever," Chuck says.

"No one said writing poetry was easy," Louie informs him.

Chuck sighs. "That game looks cool," he says to Ralphie. "Can I play?"

"I don't think it would be fair," Ralphie says. "I'm the high scorer."

"Don't worry. I'm a quick learner," Chuck says, grabbing a controller. Ralphie sighs and resets the game.

"Prepare to be *verminated*," he says.

"Aha!" Louie says about an hour later. "I think I'm finished!"

"Me, too," says Chuck. He's entering his initials as the new high scorer. "*Verminator* was way easier than I thought. Sorry I beat you all those times, Ralphie."

"Not as sorry as I am," Ralphie grumbles, shoving away the controller.

Louie stands up. "Get a load of this," he says.

Dear Fluffy,

Don't you know how Sporty I am,
how cool I am,
how popular in school I am?
Won't you give me a glance?
If we found romance.....
.....you would be so lucky.
    — with love, Chucky.

"Not bad," Chuck says. "But my name is Chuck, not Chucky."

"It's called *poetic license*," Louie informs him. "Don't worry, Fluffy

will love it. Girls love mushy poetry. It's, like, a fact."

"She'd better," Chuck says. "I can't take much more of this romance stuff."

"Me neither," Ralphie grumbles.

- 5 -

OOPS

The next day is Saturday. After Louie works at the arcade with his friends, he meets Chuck at the park.

"OK, here's the poem. I copied it on my dad's good paper, and I made sure to make the handwriting extra messy, like yours," Louie says.

"I hope this won't take long," Chuck says. "My game starts in a few minutes."

"Fancy meeting you here!" says Millicent. "We came to watch you."

"And cheer you on!" says Tiny.

"There's something he has to do first," says Louie. He points Chuck in the direction of the community garden.

"Why is he going over there?" Millicent asks.

"Romance is about to bloom," Louie says. He rubs his hands together.

"Hi, Fluffy," says Chuck.

"Oh, hi . . ." says Fluffy.

"Chuck. My name is Chuck," he says.

"Hmm," Fluffy says. "I don't think these strawberries are ripe yet. Do you?"

"How should I know?" Chuck says. "Look, I made you something."

"I'm kind of busy right now," says Fluffy.

"But my game is starting any minute," Chuck informs her. He waves the paper. "I need you to look at it *now*."

"OK, fine," Fluffy says.

She takes the poem from Chuck. But she forgets to take off her gardening gloves. What was once a poem is now a muddy, unreadable mess.

"Oops," Fluffy says.

"Hey!" says Chuck. "Louie—I mean, *I* worked hard on that!"

"I'm sorry. What did it say?" Fluffy asks.

Chuck tries to remember. "Uh . . . it was about how cool I am," he says. "A lot of the words even rhymed."

"That's . . . nice," Fluffy says. She goes back to considering her strawberries.

"Hey, is the game gonna start soon?" Millicent asks.

"I hope so. This sign is *heavy*," says Tiny.

"Clearly, Project Fluffy needs to kick things up a notch for Phase Three," Louie decides. "Game ON."

– 6 –
LOVE STINKS

Phase Three starts on Monday.

"Jeez, this bouquet was expensive," Chuck says.

"Don't worry. It'll be worth it," says Louie. "Girls love flowers. It's, like, a fact."

But when they get to the lunch table with the bouquet, Fluffy wrinkles her nose.

"*ACHOO! ACHOO!* Can you get those flowers away from me? I'm allergic," Fluffy says, sniffling. "That's why my garden is strictly fruits and vegetables."

Chuck looks at Louie. Louie shrugs.

"I guess I can give these to my mom," Chuck says. "I did forget her birthday last week."

Chad takes a bite of his ice-cream sandwich.

"It's not a gift if you can't eat it," he says.

"Hmm . . . that gives me an idea," says Louie.

Phase Four starts on Tuesday.

"And I thought flowers were pricey," says Chuck.

"You didn't have to get so much candy," says Louie, peering into the bag. "It looks like you bought the whole store."

"Well, I don't know what Fluffy likes, so I just bought what I like," Chuck says. "And I like a *lot* of candy."

"She'll be sweet on you in no time," says Louie. "Girls love candy. It's, like, a fact."

"Did I hear that you boys brought candy to school? You know that's against the rules," says Mr. Ferretti, their teacher. "I'm going to have to confiscate that bag, Mr. Wood."

"Great," Chuck says. "There goes all my savings for a new baseball glove."

"Don't worry," Louie says. "My next idea won't cost a thing."

Phase Five starts on Wednesday.

"You need to show her how strong you are," Louie says. "Girls like strong guys."

"Let me guess," Chad says. "Is it, like, a fact?"

"You're catching on," says Louie.

Chuck sighs and rolls up his sleeves.

"Do you ladies need HELP?" he asks the cafeteria workers, a little too loudly. "I'd be glad to TAKE OUT THE TRASH."

"That's kind of you, Chuck," says Mrs. Weasler.

Chuck lifts the trash bags over his head. He looks in Fluffy's direction and grins.

"My hero," says Millicent.

"What a guy," says Tiny.

"What a *show-off*," says Fluffy. She takes a sip from her carrot juice, then goes back to her gardening notebook.

"Well," says Louie, crossing off another plan on his clipboard. "There goes that idea."

"Don't forget—your entries for the poetry contest are due by the end of the school day tomorrow!" Principal Otteriguez announces to the lunchroom.

"*I* haven't forgotten," says Ralphie, giving his brother a look.

"Did you say something?" Louie asks.

"Nothing important," says Ralphie. *"Clearly."*

"I have an idea," says Tiny. He turns to Millicent. "There's still time for us to enter the poetry contest together. I can write something about how awesome we think Chuck is."

"And I can illustrate it! Genius!" says Millicent. She and Tiny high-five each other. "We'd better get started right away."

"You're going to write a poem about Chuck? You can't tell a *boy* you think he's cool," Chad informs Tiny as he polishes off his second chocolate pudding. "Not if *you're* a boy."

"Why not?" asks Tiny.

"I don't know," says Chad. "You just can't."

"I give you my dessert every day because I think *you're* cool," Tiny informs him.

"You do?" Chad says. He hesitates . . . then pats Tiny on the back. "Actually, I think you're pretty cool, too."

"Thanks," says Tiny.

Chad takes another bite of pudding.

"Mmm," says Chad. "Cool, and sweet . . . and *chocolatey*."

"Why do I think we're not talking about me anymore?" Tiny says.

"I like you a lot, Tiny," says Chad. "But I *love* pudding."

On the way home from school, Chuck can barely carry his books.

"My arms are killing me from lugging those trash bags, and now

I smell like garbage," he says. "Love *stinks!*"

"I think that might just be you," says Ralphie, sniffing.

"This is a *private* conversation," Louie reminds his brother.

"Don't worry, I know the drill," he says, glaring at them.

"I have another idea," Louie tells Chuck.

"What phase are we on now? Seven? Eight?" Chuck asks.

"Phase Six," Louie says. "This one will *definitely* work. I just need to turn the poem I wrote about Fluffy into a song, and then you can appear under her window and serenade her!"

"Serenade?" says Chuck.

"Girls love to be serenaded," Louie informs him. "It's, like, a fact."

"Sneaking around in the dark under someone's window? Sounds more like *trespassing*," says Ralphie.

"He's right," Chuck says, throwing up his hands. "You know, I might stink right now, but your advice is *really* garbage, Louie. See you around."

"Wait! I thought we were friends!" Louie calls. But Chuck has already stormed off.

"Good riddance," says Ralphie.

"You're just jealous because Chuck is cool and he wants to hang out with me and not you," Louie says.

"He's not a real friend," Ralphie says. "He was just using you to get to Fluffy."

"Well, next time I need your two cents, I'll ask for it," says Louie.

"Oh, yeah?" says Ralphie, stomping off. "We'll see about that."

THINKING
AND
SCRIBBLING

Don't forget — entries for the poetry contest are due after school today by five o'clock!" Principal Otteriguez announces at lunch.

"Uh-oh," says Louie. "We'd better start working on our poem."

"We?" says Ralphie. "This time, you're on your own, big brother."

"But I'm fresh out of ideas," Louie says.

"Maybe because you spent the whole week coming up with ideas for *Chuck,*" Ralphie reminds him.

Louie tries to think of ideas all afternoon. He's still drawing a blank when the final bell rings.

"I still have until five. Maybe you guys could help me brainstorm?" Louie says after school.

"Poetry? Blech," says Chad.

"Fluffy, can you help?" Louie says.

"I have to go water my plants," she says.

"How about you guys?" Louie asks Millicent and Tiny.

"We have our own poem to finish," says Millicent.

"Plus, we're really mad at you, Louie Ratso," says Tiny.

"Why?" asks Louie. "What did I do?"

"Because of you, Chuck isn't sitting with us at lunch anymore," says Tiny.

"Now we have to admire him from all the way across the cafeteria again!" says Millicent.

"But I can't do all of this by myself!" Louie says.

He stays after school thinking and scribbling, scribbling and thinking. But nothing sounds right.

It's so much harder working alone, he realizes. *And a lot less fun.*

– 8 –

TOUGH WEEK

You're late," Big Lou says when Louie finally gets home.

"I was trying to write something in time to enter the poetry contest," Louie says. "But nothing I came up with was good enough."

Ralphie is already finished with his dinner. "May I have some ice cream?" he asks.

"You may," says Big Lou. He turns back to Louie. "Your meatball grinder is cold now. Do you want me to heat it up?"

"No, that's OK," Louie says. The grinder is cold and a little soggy, but he's too hungry to care.

"You look tired," says Big Lou.

"I've been trying to help a kid at school get a girl to notice him," Louie says. "But Project Fluffy has been a disaster."

"Maybe because Fluffy is a *person* and not a project," Ralphie says, taking a bite of rocky road.

"Ralphie is right. Women aren't projects, or objects," Big Lou notes. "When I first met your mom, I really wanted her to like me, so I figured out what she liked."

"She liked to laugh and to sing," says Louie.

"And she liked strawberry ice cream," says Ralphie. "That's my second favorite, after rocky road."

"That's all true. And she also liked bird-watching," says Big Lou.

"She used to wear binoculars," says Ralphie. "And carry around that little notebook."

"That's where she'd write about the birds she saw," says Louie.

Mama and the boys—Big City Park

"On our first date, we went to the Big City Park and watched the birds," says Big Lou.

"You watched birds?" says Ralphie. "*Bo*-ring!"

"I thought it would be, but it was actually kind of interesting," says Big Lou. "And then, of course, I took her out for strawberry ice cream."

"I bet the ice cream sealed the deal," said Ralphie.

"What sealed the deal came after the ice cream," says Big Lou. "That's when I told her how much I liked her."

"You told her you liked her *to her face?*" Ralphie says.

"It felt pretty great to say it, actually," Big Lou says. "I wish I'd told your mom how I felt about her more often. I'm glad I can tell you boys how much I love you every day."

"I love you, too, Dad," says Louie.

"Me, too," says Ralphie. "Every day."

As Louie eats his soggy sandwich, he thinks about Mama Ratso. Talking about her and all the things she liked makes him feel good. It almost seems as if she's there with them, laughing and eating ice cream.

9

FRIENDS

At the end of the day on Friday, the whole school assembles in the auditorium.

"I'm proud to introduce the winners of the First Annual Peter Rabbit Elementary School Poetry Contest," Mr. Otteriguez announces. "First prize goes to . . . Millicent Stanko and Tiny Crawley, for their illustrated poem, 'Chuck Steals Home'!"

"SQUEEEE!" exclaim Millicent and Tiny as they high-five each other. After Tiny reads his poem, Millicent shows everyone her drawings.

"They really do make a good team," Louie admits.

"And now, second prize," Mr. Otteriguez announces. "Congratulations to Velma Diggs, for her poem, 'The Hole World'!"

"Whoa, that was deep," Chad says when Velma finishes reading.

"And third prize goes to . . . Ralphie Ratso, for his poem, 'Friends'!"

"What?" Louie says.

"Ahem," Ralphie says. Then he starts reading.

Friends
a rhyming poem by R. Ratso

When it comes to the friends of Ralphie Ratso,
here are some things you should know:

TINY is funny, and really nice.
He's one of my favorite mice.

MILLICENT has amazing hair, a cool
attitude, and artistic flair.

You might think all CHAD does is eat,
but I know he can also be funny and sweet.

FLUFFY'S favorite is anything green —
She's the best gardener I've ever seen!

LOUIE is my brother. He's super smart.
I really miss him when we're apart.

MY FRIENDS are the best. I love them so.

I'm the luckiest rat I know.

"That's so beautiful," says Tiny.

"Is someone cutting onions in here?" asks Chad, wiping a tear from his eye.

"Wow," Louie says after the assembly ends. "You wrote that poem?"

"I had a lot of free time this week," Ralphie reminds him.

"Most of what I tried to write was pretty bad," Louie admits. "Except for this part." He hands over his clipboard.

Today I am mizerable
and down on my luck.

I feel bad I ignored Ralphie
and spent all my time
with Chuck.

As long as we're together
I never feel stuck.

"All that time I was trying to figure out what Chuck needed to get Fluffy's attention, and I wasn't paying attention to what *you* needed," Louie says. "I'm really sorry."

"I'm sorry I didn't help *you* when you needed it," Ralphie says. "I think I was jealous, but not because Chuck wanted to hang out with you. Because *you* wanted to hang out with *Chuck*."

"Well, it turned out you didn't need anyone's help. You're a really good writer," Louie says.

"But I only won third place," Ralphie says. "The third-place gift certificate isn't enough to buy two skateboards."

"You should just buy one for yourself. You earned it," Louie suggests.

"Nah, it won't be as much fun riding without you," says Ralphie. His eyes brighten. "But you know, *Verminator 2* is coming out soon. Maybe I'll buy it for us, along with a fresh bag of Happy Puffs."

"As long as we're together, I'm happy enough," Louie says.

"As long as we're together and I'm the high scorer again!" says Ralphie.

"Hey, guys," says Chuck Wood. "What's up, Millicent? Hi, Tiny."

"Oh, hey," says Millicent, pretending not to care.

"Whatever," says Tiny.

"I just wanted to thank you for that poem. I'm really nervous about my game tomorrow, so it's nice to know you're thinking of me," he says.

"It was nothing," says Millicent.

"Whatever," Tiny says again.

"I really liked your drawings of me, Millicent," Chuck says. "You made me look like a real baseball star!"

Millicent blushes. "I just draw what I see," she says.

"And Tiny, I loved the sporty details you put in the poem," Chuck says.

"I had a *ball* writing it," Tiny admits.

"You guys really get me," Chuck says. "Maybe I'll see you tomorrow at the game?"

"Definitely," says Millicent.

"Sure!" says Tiny.

"Don't forget to bring your Chuck signs," Chuck says.

As Chuck walks away, Millicent and Tiny look at each other.

"SQUEEEE!" they say.

As he watches the scene unfold between Chuck and Millicent and Tiny, Louie thinks about his conversation with Ralphie, and what Big Lou said at dinner the night before. He thinks about Mama Ratso and her bird-watching notebook . . . which was *a lot* like Fluffy's gardening notebook. Then he gets an idea, too.

"Wait, Chuck," he says. "I just thought of something nice you could do for Fluffy, just like Millicent and Tiny did for you."

Chuck rolls his eyes. "I'm done with Project Fluffy," he says.

"Me, too," says Louie. "I spent all my time trying to find a way for you to get Fluffy's attention, because that's what *you* wanted. But I wasn't thinking about Fluffy at all. When you like someone, you need to pay attention to what *they* want."

"OK," Chuck says, sighing. "I'm listening."

Louie whispers in his ear.

10

PIZZA, OR . . . SALAD

Finally," Fluffy says.

That Saturday afternoon, her strawberries look perfectly red and ripe. But just as she's about to pick them, she hears a voice.

"Hey," says Chuck.

"Oh. Hi, Chuck," says Fluffy.

"I know you're busy with your garden, but I just wanted to bring you . . . this bouquet," he says. "Since you're allergic to flowers, I thought you could plant these seeds instead."

"Wow!" Fluffy says, smiling. "This is so . . . thoughtful."

"I just wanted you to know I like you," says Chuck. "If you like me, too, maybe sometime we could go out for pizza, or . . . salad?"

"Chuck," says Fluffy, "I think I could like you as a friend. But my heart belongs to my garden."

"OK," says Chuck. "You know, the more I think about it, my heart really belongs to baseball."

"Friends?" asks Fluffy.

"Definitely," says Chuck. "Friends."

They shake paws. Then Fluffy looks over at the baseball field.

"Um, speaking of baseball, isn't your game about to start?" she asks.

"Thanks for reminding me!" Chuck says. He grabs his glove and runs off.

"I didn't know you were all coming to watch the game," Millicent says.

"I bought an extra foam finger, if anyone wants it," says Tiny.

"We're having a picnic," Louie says.

"And maybe watching some birds," says Big Lou.

"I'm just here for the food," Chad explains. "Well, that and the company."

"Leave some room for dessert, gang—I have fresh-picked straw-berries," says Fluffy.

"I'm feeling inspired," says Ralphie. "Ahem. . . ."

"I love picnics, and baseball,
and sunny weather.
But most of all,
I love when we're all together."

"Game ON!" says Louie.